ELEPHANT

For LF
with love from
J. A.

For Emma and Catherine Rolla,
with thanks
T. H.

The author and publisher wish to thank
Martin Jenkins for his invaluable assistance in the
preparation of this book and the Kikaya family for
being so generous with their time and advice.

Text copyright © 1993 by Judy Allen
Illustrations copyright © 1993 by Tudor Humphries

First U.S. edition 1993

First published in Great Britain in 1992 by Walker Books Ltd., London.

Library of Congress Cataloging-in-Publication Data

Allen, Judy.
Elephant / by Judy Allen ; illustrated by Tudor Humphries.—
1st U.S. ed.
Summary: When Hannah finds an ivory necklace that belonged to her
great-grandmother, it gives her dreams; and she knows she must make
restitution to the elephants for their suffering caused by the ivory trade.
ISBN 1-56402-069-X (trade)
[1. Elephants—Fiction. 2. Rare animals—Fiction. 3. Ivory industry—Fiction.
4. Wildlife conservation—Fiction. 5. Blacks—Africa—Fiction.]
I. Humphries, Tudor, ill. II. Title.
PZ7.A4273El   1993
[E]—dc20   92-54407

10 9 8 7 6 5 4 3 2 1

Printed in Hong Kong

The pictures in this book were done in watercolor.

Candlewick Press
2067 Massachusetts Avenue
Cambridge, Massachusetts 02140

ELEPHANT

by
Judy Allen

illustrated by
Tudor Humphries

CANDLEWICK PRESS
CAMBRIDGE, MASSACHUSETTS

"I don't know what to do with this," said Hannah's mother. Her voice echoed strangely inside the cupboard she was tidying.

"What is it?" said Hannah.

Her mother turned away from the cupboard holding a small pouch made of soft leather. She loosened the drawstring at the top and turned the bag upside down. Something fell out, with a clatter, onto the table beside Hannah's father. He leaned forward to look at it. "Oh, that," he said. "I thought you'd gotten rid of that years ago."

Hannah hurried over to see.

Lying on the table was a necklace the color of thick, rich cream. It had twenty-two beads the same size, and one much larger bead in the center. Each bead was marked with a pattern of swirling shapes so that it looked almost like a flower bud.

What made it really special, though, was that on either side of the large bead was a small carved elephant, with a smaller elephant behind it, and a tiny elephant behind that. The leading elephants had their foreheads pressed to the large bead, as if they were holding it in place, and each of the following elephants had its trunk twined around the tail of the elephant in front.

"It's beautiful!" said Hannah.

"It belonged to your great-grandmother," said her mother. "But she never wore it. She left it to your grandmother, and your grandmother gave it to me."

"And neither of you ever wore it, either," said Hannah's father. "I'm surprised you kept it when none of you liked it."

"But it's perfect," said Hannah, stroking the little elephants with her fingertip. She touched their delicate ears and sharp tusks. She could even see the toenails on their strange round feet. "Why don't you like it?"

"It's made of ivory," said Hannah's father. "It's made from elephant tusks." He looked as if he was going to say something more, but her mother interrupted him. "Your great-grandfather gave it to your great-grandmother," she said. "He had it made for her."

Hannah picked it up and held it around her neck. "Why didn't she wear it?" she said.

Her mother took it gently away from her and put it back in its bag. "Because it gave her dreams," she said.

"What dreams?" said Hannah with interest.

Her father shifted in his chair. "She's old enough to be told," he said.

"There's nothing to tell," said her mother. "It's all in the past. Hannah, it's your bath time. Off you go." And she refused to say any more.

When Hannah went to bed, she thought about the necklace until she went to sleep. She thought about it the next day, too, and the day after that. On the third day, she went to the cupboard to see if it was still there. It was.

"They won't tell me about you," Hannah whispered to the six little elephants in their circle of beads. "So you'll have to tell me yourselves. I'm going to put you under my pillow and see if you give *me* dreams, like you gave my great-grandmother."

That night she went to sleep with her fingers closed around the soft leather pouch that held the necklace.

When it began, the dream was full of a kind of dust storm, a golden gritty cloud through which Hannah could just see the black branches of twisted, thorny trees. Then, as her dream-self watched, she saw that something was moving slowly behind the drifting dust.

At first, she was not frightened. She felt sure that she knew what she was going to see when the dust lifted, and she was right. A great gray elephant was treading slowly toward her, past the trees. It was followed by a small elephant, which walked less steadily and more lightly than its huge mother.

In the dream, everything was silent. Hannah could not hear the wind that had pushed the dust cloud away, nor the footfalls of the elephants, and when the big female stopped

right in front of her, she could not hear the trumpeting
sound that she knew must be coming from the raised trunk.

That was when she began to be frightened—because she
knew that the elephant was very angry with her; angry and
hurt and puzzled all at the same time.

She wanted to ask what was the matter, but although
she opened her mouth, she could not make any words
come out. Then, to her surprise, she found that she
somehow understood what the elephant was telling her.

At that moment there was a loud bang—the elephant shuddered and disappeared—and Hannah woke screaming.

"Hannah, it's all right," said her father, hurrying into her room. "It was only a car backfiring."

Hannah listened as the car rattled along the road outside—and let out one more bang as it turned the corner.

"But it hurt the elephant," said Hannah, still half asleep.

"You were dreaming," said her mother, coming into the room behind her father and sitting on the edge of the bed. "Everything's all right."

Hannah took the leather pouch from under her pillow and emptied the necklace out of it. "The elephant doesn't think it's all right," she said. "Why won't you tell me about this?"

Her mother said, "Oh, Hannah, you shouldn't have taken it."

But her father said, "Your great-grandfather was a hunter. He shot elephants and sold their tusks to ivory dealers. He kept part of one tusk for himself, and when he could afford it, he paid a craftsman to make this necklace."

"You mustn't think badly of him," said her mother. "He did it to support his family."

"I have to go and see the elephants," said Hannah.

"You've often seen elephants," said her mother.

"They weren't angry with me then," said Hannah.

"They're not angry with you now," said her mother. "This necklace was made years before you were even born."

"We stole the ivory," said Hannah. "That's what the big elephant in the dream wanted me to know. I need to see them and say we're sorry."

"We'd planned to go to the game reserve for the holiday weekend," said her father. "You'll have to wait until then. Meanwhile, let's put this thing back in the cupboard while we decide what to do with it."

Hannah didn't dream the dream again, but she didn't
forget it, either, and when the holiday weekend arrived
she went back to the cupboard and took the necklace out
of its pouch. It didn't look beautiful anymore. It was not
white like cream; it was white like bone and the dainty
elephants seemed to mock the powerful animal who had
died for their sake. Hannah slipped it into the pocket
of her jeans.

The reserve stretched for mile upon mile in every
direction—not a garden, not a park, just a piece of Africa
where people were not allowed to hunt, and where the
animals lived, and died, in their own way.

They saw gazelles, zebras, wildebeests, and, in the far
distance, a pride of lions resting under a thorn tree—but no
elephants. At least, not until the next day, when they joined
a group of other visitors in a large hide near a water hole.

Soon, the elephants began to arrive, plodding through
the undergrowth and wading into the water to drink.

The ranger in charge pointed out different members
of the herd. He didn't trouble to speak quietly—the
elephants were used to the hide and were not bothered
by the people who stared, and exclaimed, from inside it.

"You can sense how heavy they are," said Hannah's
mother, "just by looking at them."

"They are the largest land mammals in the world," said
the ranger.

"However often I see them," said Hannah's
father, "they always come as a surprise. They look so
ancient—even the young ones look ancient."

"They've been on the earth for thousands of years," said
the ranger.

Hannah said nothing. She just watched—and sometimes
she touched the ivory necklace, where it lay in her pocket.

First, the elephants drank. When they had drunk enough, the younger ones began to play, pushing each other over and climbing on each other like puppies. Then some of them used their trunks like water pistols, and one of the adults sank to its knees and almost disappeared beneath the surface.

"You see," whispered Hannah's mother, "the elephants are having fun. They're not angry with you."

"No," said Hannah. "But the one in my dream isn't here."

"Oh, Hannah," said her mother, "you don't expect us to visit every elephant in Africa, do you?"

Hannah didn't know what to say, so she said nothing.

She was quiet while the ranger drove them back to the lodge, and quiet as they traveled back through the reserve in their own car, on their way home.

What happened next happened without any warning.

They were driving along a rough track, between dense stands of trees and underbrush. Suddenly, a great she-elephant pushed through the branches and leaves to their left, trunk raised, roaring with rage.

Hannah's father braked so suddenly that the car's engine choked—and stopped.

The elephant was only about ten feet away—towering over the car.

"It's her," whispered Hannah to herself, and she was so frightened she thought she might be sick.

"It's because of her calf," said Hannah's mother. She pointed to the opposite side of the track where a small elephant stood, watching them uncertainly. "We're between her and her calf."

The grown elephant swayed forward and let out another trumpeting call, full of fury and menace.

"I don't know what to do," said Hannah's father, clenching his hands on the steering wheel until the knuckles looked as though they would push through the skin. "If I restart the engine, the noise may enrage her more."

"But I know what to do," said Hannah to herself, and she pulled the ivory necklace out of the pocket of her jeans.

"If she attacks the car," said Hannah's mother in a small voice, "would she be able to crush it?"

"Yes," said Hannah's father, "in seconds."

Then, before anyone could stop her, Hannah
wound down the window beside her and threw the
necklace as far as she could, so that it fell onto the
middle of the track, in front of the car. Then she
closed the window quickly.

"What did you do!" cried her father.

"Start the car!" said her mother. "We'll have to
risk it now!"

"No, wait," said her father.

The big elephant turned her head away for a moment, distracted by the thing that had fallen on the track. At the same time, the baby elephant trotted across in front of the car, curious and unafraid, to have a closer look. It pushed the necklace with its trunk—then picked it up and trotted to its mother's side. She lowered her trunk to stroke her

calf and then pushed it gently ahead of her, into the safety
of the underbrush.

At the last moment, she glanced briefly back at the car.
This time she did not look angry at all. Then both
elephants disappeared among the trees.

In silence, Hannah's father started the car and drove on slowly.

"Your trick worked, Hannah," he said at last. "But you took a big risk."

"The necklace is lost," said her mother. "I didn't see whether the young elephant took it or dropped it, but I don't feel like going back to look!"

"It isn't lost," said Hannah, and she was smiling. "I gave it back. It was my great-grandmother's necklace, but it was made from her great-grandmother's tusks."

"I'm glad you threw it away," said her mother, "especially for such a good cause—but no one can ever know which elephant it came from."

"I know," said Hannah. "I know because she told me. In my dream."

ELEPHANT FACT SHEET

There are two species of elephants alive today. The rarer of the two is the Asian elephant, which lives in the jungles and forests of the Indian region and Southeast Asia. This elephant is quite often domesticated and is used for dragging heavy logs out of the forest. There are probably about 40,000 Asian elephants left and their numbers are decreasing, although slowly. African elephants, like the ones in the story, live in savannas, woodlands, and forests in many parts of Africa. There are far more of them— around 600,000—than there are Asian elephants, but their numbers are decreasing much more quickly than previously. Only fifteen years ago there were twice as many as there are today.

WHAT ARE THE DANGERS FOR ELEPHANTS?

People kill elephants for their ivory, which is used to make jewelry and other precious objects. People also kill elephants because they damage their crops, and for their meat and skins. In addition, the forests are being cut down and the savannas and woodlands turned into farmland, leaving the elephants with fewer places to live.

IS ANYONE HELPING ELEPHANTS?

Yes. Governments in Africa and Asia have set up many national parks and reserves where elephants can live, and several conservation organizations have helped in this. In 1989 the Convention on International Trade in Endangered Species made trade in elephant ivory illegal in order to discourage poaching.

ARE EFFORTS TO HELP ELEPHANTS SUCCEEDING?

In part. Some of the parks and reserves where elephants live are well protected and the elephants are safe there, but in others there are not enough guards, and elephants are still being poached. The ban on the ivory trade has helped decrease the number of elephants being killed, but has not stopped all killing.

IS THERE ANYTHING YOU CAN DO?

Yes. You can send any specific questions you have about elephants and what's being done to save them to the address below. Please be sure to included a stamped, self-addressed envelope.

The Elephant Research Foundation
106 E. Hickory Grove
Bloomfield Hills, MI 48034
USA